W9-CCQ-120

for Craig from Natalie

for Matt & Sarah from Hilary

# A NOTE TO PARENTS

When your children are ready to "step into reading," giving them the right books—and lots of them—is as crucial as giving them the right food to eat. **Step into Reading Books** present exciting stories and information reinforced with lively, colorful illustrations that make learning to read fun, satisfying, and worthwhile. They are priced so that acquiring an entire library of them is affordable. And they are beginning readers with an important difference—they're written on four levels.

**Step 1 Books,** with their very large type and extremely simple vocabulary, have been created for the very youngest readers. **Step 2 Books** are both longer and slightly more difficult. **Step 3 Books,** written to mid-second-grade reading levels, are for the child who has acquired even greater reading skills. **Step 4 Books** offer exciting nonfiction for the increasingly proficient reader.

Children develop at different ages. **Step into Reading Books,** with their four levels of reading, are designed to help children become good—and interested—readers *faster*. The grade levels assigned to the four steps—preschool through grade 1 for Step 1, grades 1 through 3 for Step 2, grades 2 and 3 for Step 3, and grades 2 through 4 for Step 4—are intended only as guides. Some children move through all four steps very rapidly; others climb the steps over a period of several years. These books will help your child "step into reading" in style!

# The Best Little

*Library of Congress Cataloging-in-Publication Data:* Standiford, Natalie. The best little monkeys in the world.
(Step into reading. A Step 2 book) SUMMARY: When their parents go out to a party, two little monkeys make
mischief while their baby-sitter thinks they are being good. [1. Monkeys—Fiction. 2. Baby-sitters—Fiction
3. Behavior—Fiction] I. Knight, Hilary, ill. II. Title. III. Series: Step into reading. Step 2 book.
PZ7.S78627Be 1987 [E] 86-15425 ISBN: 0-394-88616-X (trade); 0-394-98616-4 (lib. bdg.)

Manufactured in the United States of America        17  18  19  20

STEP INTO READING is a trademark of Random House, Inc.

# Monkeys in the World

A Step 2 Book

By Natalie Standiford
Illustrated by Hilary Knight

Random House 🏠 New York

Text copyright © 1987 by Random House, Inc. Illustrations copyright © 1987 by Hilary Knight. All rights reserved under International and Pan-American Copyright Conventions. Published in the United States by Random House, Inc., New York, and simultaneously in Canada by Random House of Canada Limited, Toronto.

Mama Monkey was wearing
her best dress.

Papa Monkey was putting on
his new striped tie.

They were going to a party—
a party just for grown-up monkeys.

"Judy is coming to baby-sit,"
Mama told Marvin and Mary.
Marvin and Mary
jumped up and down.
"Hooray!" they cried.

"Judy lets us do anything we want,"
Marvin said to Mary.

"Yes," said Mary.

"We can have shakes for dinner.
We can play all we want.
We can stay up late
and watch TV!"

Just then the doorbell rang.

It was Judy.

Marvin and Mary hid.

"Boo!" they cried.

"Now, be good,"
said Mama Monkey.

"They are always good,"
said Judy.

"They are the best little
monkeys in the world."

Judy picked up the phone.

She called her friend Ann.

Mary asked,

"Can we make dinner, Judy?"

Judy stopped talking

to her friend.

"Sure!" she said.

"You two are the best little

monkeys in the world."

Marvin and Mary went to the kitchen.

"Banana shake time!"

said Marvin.

"Let's make BIG shakes."

Mary put ten bananas
in the blender.
She put in lots of milk
and lots of ice cream.
Then Marvin pressed
the button.

Whirr! Splash!

Banana shake was

all over the kitchen!

Banana shake was all over

Marvin and Mary, too.

They drank the rest of the shake.

"Yum!" said Mary.

"This is good," Marvin said.

"But I am all sticky now.

Let's take a bath—

a bubble bath!"

Marvin went in

and said to Judy,

"May we take our bath now?"

Judy was talking

to her friend Ellen.

Judy put her hand over the phone.

"Sure," she said.

"You are the best little monkeys

in the world."

Marvin turned on the water.

Mary put in lots of bubble bath.

The tub began to fill up.

"This takes so long,"
said Marvin.
"Let's go out and play.
When we come back,
the tub will be full."

Marvin and Mary
played on their jungle gym.
"It is fun to play at night,"
said Mary.

But it was dark.

Marvin slipped.

So did Mary.

Splash!

They fell in a mud puddle!

"Now we really need a bath,"

said Mary.

They went back to the house.
They left a trail of mud.

"What is coming out of the house?"
cried Mary.

It was bubbles!

Lots and lots of bubbles!

Bubbles were everywhere.

Marvin turned off the water.

He and Mary got into the tub.

"We made a big mess,"

said Mary.

"But I love bubble baths!"

Marvin and Mary took a very long bath.

Then they put on their pajamas.

They went to see Judy.

"May we watch TV now, Judy?"

asked Mary.

Judy put down the phone.

"Sure," she said.

"You really are the best little

monkeys in the world."

Marvin turned on the TV.

"Look!" he said. "A spooky show!"

Mary said,

"Mama does not like us

to watch spooky shows."

"Do not be a baby,"

said Marvin.

They watched the spooky show.

It was about two children.

The children were in an old house.

A big ghost was about to grab them!

"This show is too spooky,"

said Marvin.

"I am scared."

Mary said,

"I am scared too."

They hugged each other.

"Judy! Judy! We are scared!" they cried.

ON-OFF     VOLUME     FUR-TONE

Judy was not talking
on the phone now.
She was fast asleep.

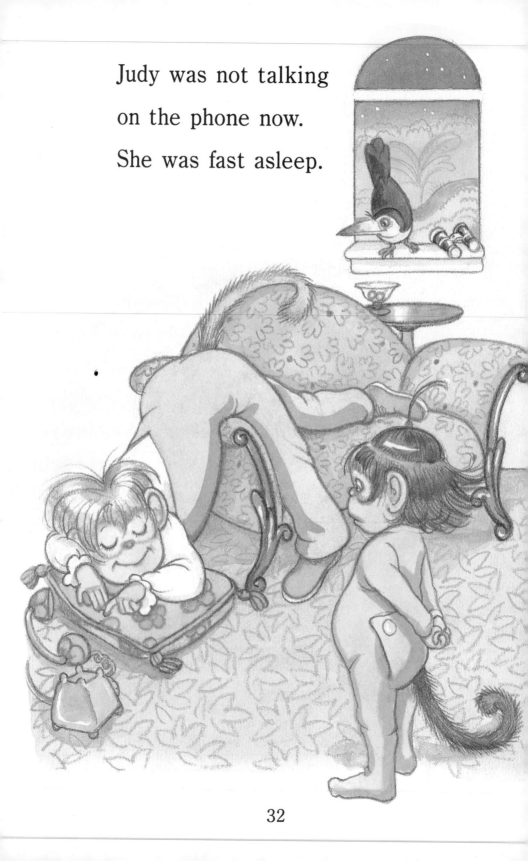

Marvin saw the clock.

It said 11 o'clock.

"Mama and Papa
will be home soon,"
he said.

Then Mary saw all the mess.
"Oh, no!
Mama and Papa
will be very mad.
We must clean up
before they get home."

So Marvin and Mary
got a mop and a pail.

They cleaned up
the mud on the floor.

They cleaned up
the bubbles
in the bathroom.

38

They cleaned up
the banana shake
in the kitchen.

They put away the mop
and the pail.
"That was hard work,"
said Marvin.
"But we are done."

Marvin and Mary went to their room.

"I am very tired," said Mary.

"Me too," said Marvin.

They got into
their beds.

Mary held her baby doll.

Soon they were fast asleep.

A little later
Judy woke up.
"Mary? Marvin?"
she called.
"Where are you?"

She ran to their room.
"Well, what do you know.
They went to bed
all by themselves!"
said Judy.

Soon Mama and Papa came home.

"It was a lovely party,"

said Mama.

"Were Marvin and Mary good?"

"Oh, they were wonderful!"
said Judy.
"I always say
they are the best little monkeys
in the world!"

"Good night!"